ONE BREATH
69m
70m
71m
72m
Jordan Z. Lowe

To Mum, Dad, my brothers and my sisters, my nephews and nieces, my loving grandparents, Dr Robyn Fried, Mrs. Theresa Goodwin, Mrs. Lynne Sherwood, Mrs. Karen Holmes, my dear friend Kate, my dear beloved Olivia and all of my friends who have supported me through writing this story.
Thank you for inspiring me to share a story with the world.

<u>Foreword</u>

My name is Jordan Z Lowe, and this is my second light novel. I will be honest, this story in its concept and design are purely experimental. The concept came to me in a dream one night. I was looking at anime art on the internet on my IPhone and then one thought led to another. I lost quite a bit of sleep that night as a result, but hey, I got a story out of it so I consider it a fair trade.

The experiment in this story is basically this· what if there was an underwater adventure story, but from start to finish, the main character was on an unrelenting timer- a timer that ticked down constantly, never letting her or the audience forget that an unhappy end might be near if she takes too long?

That's this story. I don't know how many people will like this story, or how many people will hate it. But as the old saying goes, "Nothing ventured, nothing gained."

Now, without further ado…

Let's dive in!

In loving memory of my loving nan,
Betty Valerie Lowe
1931-2019

Kaia's Diving Log

Entry 1:	9

Entry 2:	13

Entry 3:	25

Entry 4:	35

Entry 5:	46

Entry 6:	59

Entry 7:	77

Contents

Prologue

In the Pacific Ocean, there was a mysterious archipelago known as The Hidden Sapphire Archipelago, a series of islands that not only had beautiful beaches, coral reefs and ocean life worthy of art, they also held countless secrets and wonders in its oceans that couldn't be found anywhere else in the world. Ruins of long lost civilizations, countless wrecks, tombs of unfortunate victims, and even rumours of ancient, colossal creatures in the depths where many fear to tread. They were truly a wonder of the world.

But the islands themselves weren't empty either. Lush jungles and forests adorned the island in abundance, along with exotic and rare wildlife, alongside extremely adaptive colonies of native humans, both at home on the land and in the water. In the year 2020, the Hidden Sapphires were discovered by the world. This was the beginning of our story.

In the early days of outside settlement, the natives were wary but welcoming to the visitors, as the visitors took care not to abuse this wonder of the world, as they did with others in the past. Visitors from across the world looked at these islands with awe, envious of its everyday beauties and treasures. But some found even more than that in the Hidden Sapphire...like one Victor Cayden, a curious, shy, young archeologist from the Norse nation of Sweden. Victor found one treasure he was convinced he'd never find. He found love.

It was first sight. The young maiden diver of Loa, the

largest of the islands, named Lia. Gorgeous black hair, beautiful bronze tanned skin, eyes as blue as sapphires. At first she didn't think much of the young Swedish man, as the poor guy nearly drowned just watching her dive. But as they ran into each other more and more, she found his insecure, shy demeanor quite...cute. As more time passed, they talked more and more, sharing their stories and secrets as they grew closer. Eventually, much to Victor's surprise, but none of his protest, the two became more than friends.

Young Victor learned so much from Lia. One of the first things he learned was that divers from the Hidden Sapphire can dive deeper and longer on one breath than anywhere else in the world, some teenagers diving as deep as half a kilometer underwater. He also learned that these waters are an abundance of treasures and ruins, many believed to be from the creator of the Hidden Sapphire, Oci Jun or "ocean mother" in their native tongue. There was even talk of an ancient people under the deeper oceans known as "The Gilled Ones." This was why Victor came here in the first place and he wanted to see it all.

Victor expressed his wishes to see the underwater wonders, much to Lia's concern. She did not want to doubt Victor, but she knew there were outsiders willing to defile her home for profit. Knowing that, Victor made a promise.

"I want to see and share the wonders of the ocean to the world. I will never defile them for the sake of profit, or my name isn't Victor Vincent Cayden!"
Lia couldn't help but giggle at his dramatic proclamation,

but it did put her at ease. Her people also heard his plea, and were willing to give him- and ONLY him- a chance. His superiors promoted Victor to project leader of the Hidden Sapphire Undersea Expedition (HSUE), based on this sole promise he made to Lia and her people. Immensely grateful, Lia offered the only treasure she could give to Victor· her hand in marriage.

And so in the winter of 2021, they were wed together as Mr. and Mrs. Cayden. And in the summer of 2022, they gave birth to a beautiful young daughter, Kaia Cayden, who had her mother's sapphire blue eyes and bronze skin, and her father's love for mystery and discovery. And as they would later discover, a gift no other in the Hidden Sapphire had.

2026

In the summer of 2026, the Hidden Sapphires population had grown quite substantially. But thanks to outside intervention's new revolutionary floating islands, overpopulation was not an issue. Lia and Victor, along with their daughter Kaia, moved to one of these new islands, named Ark Epsilon. These artificial islands had everything the family needed· good food, drinkable water, plentiful harvests, sunshine and rain, a comfortable abode, and even an open swimming pool for the locals of the Archipelago.

The Cayden family went to the shallower family pool to take Kaia for a swimming lesson. But as the parents set up, the water beckoned Kaia, its wavy surface almost calling for her to dive in. Before, she was happy kicking along the surface, like any other young child. But this time, when her parents took her into the water, she took a huge breath and dove under at her first chance.

At first, Lia and Victor were quite scared and tried to pull her up. But they noticed as they chased after her, she swam across the bottom of the pool gracefully, like she was a sea creature. She wasn't even in any danger of drowning, as she was underwater for up to half an hour before they finally caught her...and she wasn't even out of breath. Kaia laughed and smiled, unaware of how much she frightened her parents-especially her father who was pale from fright. But they noticed. Their four-year old daughter could swim underwater with ease and hold her breath longer than most preteens from her kin. Their daughter was gifted and they nourished her love for swimming ever since.

KAIA CAYDEN

2035

As the years went by, Victor's project took shape. A new compact two-seater submarine was designed by Victor, with Lia in mind. Able to withstand enormous pressure and propel through tight spaces, it was also equipped with an airlock, for free divers to exit and enter the sub. It even came equipped with an expandable pod that could be used to establish a temporary base of operations if need be. This new exploration sub, named "Regal Glider", had Lia and Victor as its first test pilots.

The sub itself functioned perfectly up to 8000 metres of pressure, and the pod expanded to five meter diameter and fitted with an indefinite recycling oxygen supply. With the test going without a hitch, it was time to begin Victor's dream of exploring the hidden wonders of the Hidden Sapphire's waters. There was just one problem. Much to her dismay, 13 year old Kaia couldn't come along. They were all aware of Kaia's gift, but this was one risk they weren't ready to take. Leaving Kaia with the carers at Ark Epsilon, Victor and Lia left the safety of their home, to realize Victors dream. Their first stop, The Sunken Mazes.

Kaia somberly played on her own, only able to wonder what adventures her parents are having without her, while she herself was land bound, not allowed to leave the Ark without supervision. But knowing they would return in a matter of days, she put up with the boredom, counting the days. Another day passed. Another. And another. And several more after that. But Kaia's parents didn't return. None of their crew returned. No-one had even seen their ship. Kaia was getting worried, looking for any leads she could find. Listening in on the adults, she heard that even they had lost contact with her parents. As time passed, she began to fear the worst.

But Kaia didn't want to accept it. She asked for help, but they had given up on them. She asked to go out herself, but they refused to let her. She had no options left… but to take matters into her own hands. Packing some rope, a bag, and other supplies, she hatched a plan to find her parents. While no-one was looking, she hitched a ride on the anchor of a boat that was cruising over the Sunken Mazes. She held onto the anchor, making no sound and giving no indication to any bystanders as she tied the rope to the anchor, then around her waist. As the ship cruised over the Mazes, she began packing her lungs by taking slow, deep breaths. Finally, as the anchor dropped, she took one last breath and held it tight, even filling her cheeks with air. Bubbles plumed all around Kaia as the anchor rapidly sank, pinching her nose to pop her eardrums. Above all, she held her breath tight…for it was the only one she'd get in this very long dive.

Diving Log Entry 1

Time Submerged· 00 Hours· 01 Minutes· 22 Seconds

The anchor hit the seafloor sand with a dull thud, Kaia hastily untied the rope around her waist and the anchor, before putting it away in her little satchel. She surveyed the seas around her, looking for any potential trails to lead her on her search. The light from the sun above shimmered through the water, dancing on the surfaces of every leaf of seaweed, every barnacle-covered stone and every anemone swishing as a home to little finned locals. Kaia's eyes widened at the marvel around her, but she shook her head and kept going. She wasn't here to sightsee.

After a decently long period of searching the upper reefs, Kaia spotted something new· a large, worn open cavern that looked nothing like a natural formation, almost rectangular in shape. Kaia bubbled in curiousity, before taking out an underwater camera and taking a photo, then she slowly swam inside. The cavern quickly grew darker as she proceeded, but just as she was about to take out her flashlight, lights began to shimmer all around the cave walls, bathing the area in a florescent green glow. Kaia smiled behind her puffed up cheeks, putting away her flashlight and letting the algae light the way.

Up ahead, Kaia saw a fork in the road, two paths in different directions. Between the two paths, there was an artificial lamp, lighting up an odd looking wall behind it. Kaia knew she was going in the right direction, but which way to go from here? Kaia glanced long and hard at each direction, neither giving a clear indication of being a dead end or worse. There was nothing for it. She trusted her gut and went on the left path, but not before tying her rope around the lamp and carrying the other end, to leave a trail for herself in case she got lost.

Swimming onwards, she saw something new around the corner· more artificial lamps and debris, undoubtedly being the familiar design of her father's submarines. She was definitely going in the right direction, but something was off. What happened to chip off this much metal, only fifty metres inside this underwater labyrinth? Not only that, Kaia felt an eerie feeling she just couldn't shake as she swam on. She thought to herself.

"Am I being watched?"

Kaia looked in all directions, but saw no-one, not a soul. Regardless, she stroked forward past the wreckage, the path becoming smaller, no wider than ten metres. Kaia found comfort in the green glowing algae shining against her tanned skin, but she still felt uncertain about what she would find at the end of this tunnel. The rope in her hand snagged, as it

"Am I being watched...?"

appeared to hit its full length. Knowing this, Kaia tied it around the nearest rock she could find, before pressing on alone.

As the feeling she was being watched grew stronger and stronger, Kaia felt more and more uneasy. Tiny bubbles trickled from her lips as she felt worry welling up in her chest. Up ahead, the green glowing algae that covered the cave's walls suddenly ended. Now was the time to take out her flashlight. With the flick of a switch, the path ahead was now well lit, providing a minute's comfort to Kaia.

It didn't last long.

A loud boom echoed behind her, scaring her intensely as she instinctively turned around...to see the way she came blocked off by rocks. Her eyes widened as she stared at the dusty pile blocking her path to air. Then, to make things worse...from out of the dark, she saw creatures approaching. Humanoids with webbed feet and hands, hair that looked like tentacles that sprouted from their scalps, greenish skin with humanlike features and gills on their necks, carrying exotic glowing spears, all pointed at poor Kaia. She knew right away what these people were· the mythical Gilled Ones. Surrounding her, one of them, a young male adult, spoke.

"Halt! What lured you here, stranger? What is your purpose here?"

He spoke in a demanding tone, but Kaia couldn't answer. She didn't know how to talk underwater and any attempts would result in gurgled bubbling and wasted air. So she kept her lips shut, waving her hands while making a moaning sound in her throat.

"Did you not hear me, stranger? Speak!"

The man did not understand Kaia's predicament, but instead took it as defiance, despite her best attempts to appear friendly.

"Very well. If you will not talk, maybe you will learn some manners, in our prison."

"MMM?!"

Kaia's eyes widened in fright at the word "prison". But before she could react, the Gilled Ones wrapped chains around her hands and feet, then tying a rope around her cuffs before dragging her away...further away from the surface.

Diving Log Entry 2

Time Submerged. 00 Hours, 29 minutes, 58 seconds.

Against her will, Kaia was being dragged by the cuffs around her hands by her captors, the Gilled Ones. She could only go along and dread what they had planned for her. She looked at each of the Gilled Ones, each one bearing a different skin colour, along with marks, blemishes and scars, all glancing her way suspiciously.

Light began to shine ahead forcing Kaia to close her eyes for a brief moment. When she opened them again, she nearly opened her mouth in awe…for what she saw…was the Undersea Paradise. A mass of exotic houses all built on top of an old reef, along with almost skyscraper-like structures nearly touching the rocky labyrinth above that allows a little bit of sunlight to filter down. Hundreds to thousands of Gilled Ones glide across the waters like a school of fish on their daily rituals, unaware of their new visitor.

Kaia's captors dragged her along, not letting her stop to see the sights before her. Kaia felt several cold gazes on her, feeling a growing a chill in her spine. Next thing she knew, she heard the slam of a stone barred door, followed by the click of a lock. She was now in a jail cell.

Kaia sat down on the cold bench, silently trickling bubbles from her puckered lips. She put her hands on her chest, trying to keep herself calm. Collecting her thoughts, she looked around, taking in her surroundings of the cold, rocky cell with the odd barnicle on the wall. Not seeing a way out, she decided the best course would be to wait and save her breath, not making any unneccessary movement. She took out her journal from her satchel.

Kaia's Diving Log: Entry 1

I'm already in trouble down here. Diving down the cave that my parents went through, I ran into the mythical Gilled Ones, but they didn't like me. So here I am, in an underwater jail cell with nothing to do but bubble away. If I don't get out soon, I'll be waterlogged before I make it to court. My lungs are ok at the moment, but I hope I can make it out of here...somehow.

Putting away her journal, Kaia laid her head down on the bench, closing her eyes and listening to her heartbeat slowing down.

"Psst!"

Kaia heard a sound.

"Hey. Over here."

A young boy, whispering. Kaia opened her eyes and

listened. Lifting her head, she saw a hand waving near the barred window and quietly swam toward it. Holding onto the bars, she sees a Gilled One, a young boy with the same features as all the other Gilled Ones, apart from not having webbed hands and feet, with a well-groomed tentacle crown above his forehead, around her age with a concerned look.

"Hey, sorry if I scared you. Are you okay?"

Kaia was relieved to see a friendly face. But she still had the same problem as before, pointing her lips and shaking her head to tell the boy she can't talk. The boy tilted his head, but he thought for a moment and finally understood.

"Wait...you're an air breather, aren't you?"

Kaia nodded as her eyes lit up.

"You can't breathe down here, can't you?"

Kaia nodded again. Suddenly, the boy started to panic, flailing his arms, not knowing what to do.

"Oh heavens, you must be dying for a breath! You're going to drown! What am I going to do?!"

Kaia held the boy's shoulder through the bars, giving him a reassuring smile. She wanted to say that she could still hold for a long while yet. The boy calmed down with a deep sigh, before coming up with an idea.

"Wait here, I have something you can use!"

The boy dashed away at speed, leaving Kaia all alone. But he wasn't gone for long, bringing back some sort of rectangular board. He handed the board to Kaia, along with a rough-looking pencil. Kaia understood now. written communication. Wasting no time, she wrote something on the board, getting a feel for the board's rough and worn surface.

Thank you. This makes things so much easier.

The boy sighed in relief.
"So, what are you exactly?"
Kaia rubbed out her last sentence, writing a new one.

My name is Kaia. I'm a young diver from the Hidden Sapphire Archipelago. I can't talk because I'm holding my breath, but luckily I can hold my breath for several hours.

The boy was relieved to hear that. He smiled at her with curiousity.
"Kaia? My name is Olv. You're holding your breath? That's why your cheeks are like a blowfish?"
Olv pointed at Kaia's puffed up cheeks, which made Kaia giggle with a nod.

I like to pack my lungs as much as I can. Pressure isn't much of a problem for me. But I am going to run out of breath if I stay in here.

Olv's expression turned serious as he looked to the guards behind the bars.

Inuy

"See what you can do with that board. I'll try to find a way out for you in the meantime."

Olv gently clasped Kaia's hand.

"Are you going to be okay?"

Kaia smiled at Olv, she knew his care was genuine. They only just met, but she knew this young Gilled One was on her side. Kaia gave Olv the best hug she could through the bars, making the young boy blush before floating back towards the cell door, knocking it to get the guards attention.

The guards looked at her as she wrote a message to them in haste.

Please understand. I can't talk because I can't breathe down here. I'm looking for my parents. Have you seen any big metal fish?

The guards are looked at each other, quietly talking among themselves. They seemed quite serious, considering if Kaia was lying or not. Kaia held the door anxiously, her cheeks nearly squishing against the bars. After a nerve-wracking while, they turned back to her.

"We will hear what you have to say, after we summon our chieftain."

Kaia nodded in gratitude, despite their mistrust. However, they would not let Kaia out of her cell yet, once again she had to sit back and wait. She turned to the window, but Olv was no longer there. Kaia wondered if she would get a chance to thank the boy for saving her so much trouble.

The sound of heavy swimming drew Kaia's attention back to the cell door, where she was greeted by a marvelous sight! A large, heavily built male Gilled One, clad in golden plated armour, laced with exotic patterns and authentic battle damage. He gave Kaia a commanding glare, standing tall and proud with a powerful aura emanating from his very being.

"So, you are the young one from the surface? You seem far too young to dive on your own, especially where your kind is not welcome."

Kaia looked confused. She scribbled a response in haste.

I don't understand. I'm just looking for my parents. What did I do wrong?

The chieftain furrowed his brow in annoyance.

"I am Chieftain Kiav, head of the Royal Guard in Undala Padisic. You are out of your depth because your kind recently trespassed on our waters without our consent. We were at arms against them, but they didn't even try to fight back. They expressed their intentions, but their sudden intrusion and the damage their craft caused to our tunnels was unacceptable."

He must have talked about the wreckage Kaia saw on her way in. Was that really enough to irk the Gilled Ones?

"Thanks to Elder Marnik's counsel, we let them continue downward to the catacombs below, on the condition that they would not tread upon our territory again. And now, here you are, repeating their offense."

Kaia was starting to get nervous. Now that she knew the situation she was in, how would she get herself out of it? She had to think it through and choose her words carefully.

Please. I'm so sorry to have offended you, but if I can find my parents, I promise I will leave and never come back. I beg you, please give me the chance. Please don't let me drown in here.

Kaia clasped her hands together in a begging manner, her desperation sincere. The chieftain was silent, thinking for a good long while. Then he noticed the writing board that she was using, realizing that it was of his kinds making.
"Where did you get that board? Did you steal it?!"
Kaia shook her head hastily in strong denial.

No, it was given to me. A little Gilled One named Olv gave it to me a few minutes ago.

The Gilled Ones looked at each other in shock and surprise. The chieftain placed a palm on his face.
"Olv...that boy is too curious for his own good. Let's see what you told him. Guards, bring Olv to the cell! See what he can tell us about this surface youngling."
Kaia got nervous, feeling a hint of regret for saying what she said. Did she just sell her only hope out? Her heart began to race and she pat her chest to try and slow it back down, for a racing heart is very bad in freediving as it uses up air faster. Sure enough, Olv was brought to the cell door,

looking just as nervous as Kaia.

"Prince Olv, this human claims that you're trying to help her. Is that true, despite her kind's recent offenses?"

Kaia's eyes widened at the word "prince". Did she really just hear right? Olv slowly nodded. The chieftain furrowed his brow.

"May I ask your reasoning for this, my prince?"

Olv swallowed nervously. It took him a while to think of a response.

"This hu-I mean, Kaia…she bears no ill intention. She is speaking the truth…about looking for her parents."

The chieftain didn't look convinced.

"How can you be certain? For all we know, she's lying to you as well."

Kaia shook her head anxiously. Olv stood tall, putting on a brave face.

"What would she gain from lying to her captors? Tell me chieftain. What she could do to offend our kind, having brought no weapons, no armour and only the air in her lungs? If that was indeed her intentions, don't you think she would have come better prepared? If she was like the surface dwellers in the metal fish before, she would have gone with them, not by herself."

The chieftain and his men were taken aback by his response, clearly used to his shy demeanor. Kaia couldn't help but admire his newfound courage.

"I know Kaia is from the surface world, but she is not like the others that have transgressed before. All I ask is that you allow her the chance to prove her innocence."

Olv swallowed, almost choking on his next sentence.

"And furthermore, I swear on my name as Crown Prince of Undala Padisic, if she does anything, I'll incarcerate her myself until her breath expires."

Kaia's admiration turned to fear. That was a fate she truly didn't want. The thought of herself in a small cage, her cheeks and face blue from stale air with no way out, thrashing in desperation, truly filled her with fright. She knew from when she first held her breath that there would be a risk of drowning in these depths, but she never considered being imprisoned underwater of all places. But despite all these fears, all she could do was hope that Olv can get her out of the cell she was currently in.

Chieftain Kiav thought to himself for a long moment, before discussing quietly amongst his guards. He turned back to Olv and Kaia.

"Very well. We'll release her on two conditions. One. she'll be escorted in chains, which my men will hold the key until she leaves. Two. she must leave within the hour. You may take her wherever you wish in the meantime, but see that she is out of the city in an hour."

Olv thought to himself for a long moment.

"Alright, I'll accept the conditions, if your men will clear the way to the surface."

The chieftain bowed to his request.

"You have our word. We will see it done."

Olv nodded one final time.

"Alright. Open the cell, please."

The guards unlocked the cell door, letting Kaia float out slowly before putting her back in cuffs. Kaia looked at Olv worriedly. Olv mouthed something to Kaia, without saying a word.

"I'm sorry, but this is the best I can do."

Kaia read his lips and subtly nodded in understanding, letting Olv take her chains.

"So what do you plan to do with this surface youth, my Prince?"

Olv thought for a second, then snapped his fingers.

"We might look around for leads on her parents. Our kind may have seen them. Let's see...let's start with Elder Marnik."

The chieftain bowed in response.

"Very well. We will escort you, if you don't mind."

Olv shook his head. Kaia suddenly hugged Olv, causing him to blush heavily. But he knew why. He understood her gratitude and hugged back.

Diving Log Entry 3

Time Submerged. 01 Hours, 02 Minutes, 30 Seconds.

With the aid of Prince Olv, Kaia was allowed outside of her cell, with an armed escort. Kaia wrote on her board. Her hands may have been bound, but she could still write.

Can I ask what actually happened when my parents came here?

"Well, they came here by accident, using an explosive metal thing to blow their way in here. But our guards took it as an attack and took up arms."

Kaia was now beginning to understand. They must have used a depth charge to clear their path and that's when things went south. Now Kaia had to deal with the stigma they left behind, which as she would find out, would not be easy. But on the plus side, she knew where to start looking.

Who were the biggest witnesses? I'd like to ask them what they know.

"Hmm. Elder Marnik managed to stop the conflict before things got hairy. He was the only one who talked to them personally. But I'm not sure what you would get out of him. He often speaks in weird phrases."

Kaia nodded regardless. She didn't care who she needed to ask as long she had a lead. Olv signed in defeat and led Kaia on. Their route was through the local markets, where Kaia was given a treat for her eyes! Many exotic goods getting bartered and sold from enclosed bulbous stalls, some stalls more popular than others as seen from the size of the line up front. Olv caught Kaia looking around, seeing her curiousity.

"Does anything catch your eye? I can get you something if you want."

Kaia turned to Olv excitedly, her eyes glittering with a catlike smile.

"I'll...take that as a yes. So what do you like?"

Kaia took her time looking around, seeing all kinds of stones, gems, utensils and trinkets she had never seen before and had only dreamed of. Her eyes gleamed with wonder, especially one item in particular· a sapphire that gleamed flawlessly on a wristband frame. She pointed at it, looking at Olv with cutesy eyes as if to say, "Can I have it?"

Olv looked at it, swallowing nervously. He then nodded.

"S-sure. If you want it that badly."

Olv paid the cashier in oddly shaped gold coins, before receiving the bracelet, bowing in thanks. Kaia raised her wrist, wanting Olv to put it on for her. Olv blushed as he slowly fiddled with the strap, feeling her soft, warm hand. By the time he finally clicked it shut, his face was beet red, making Kaia giggle, which didn't impress the Royal Guards.

"A-anyway, s-shall we move on? The Reef Borders are

just this way. Elder Marnik should be feeding the fish now."

Kaia nodded, swimming onwards whilst following Prince Olv's lead. As they swam, Kaia could see Olv had something on his mind.
She tapped on his shoulder.

What's on your mind?

"Oh. Well, it's something I've been thinking about...How do you do it? You know, that thing you do. With your cheeks."
Kaia tilted her head, writing another question.

You mean holding my breath? Everyone can do it. It's just...I can hold mine longer than others.

Olv nodded.
"Yeah, that's what I mean. For as long I've seen you "hold your breath", most humans would be dead by now. At least, that's what I read up."

Well, you're not wrong. Most humans can barely hold their breath for five minutes. My dad can barely swim.

Scratching the back of her head with an embarrassed look, Kaia wrote.

But despite that, he loves the ocean and

everything in it. And so do I. He wants to discover the beauties of the ocean and share it with the world. He wouldn't hurt a fish, no matter what anyone says.

Olv's Royal Guards paid no heed to Kaia's words, casting disapproving looks her way. But Olv felt meaning and truth in Kaia's words. He knew she loved her parents very much, even willing to dive to the bottom of the ocean on one breath to find them. Olv simply couldn't help but smile.

"Well, you don't look like a bad person to me."

Kaia blushed on her puffed up cheeks, giving a warm smile back. They swam onwards to the Paradise's border region, the Reef Borders. Upon arrival, they were blessed with the sight of a huge reef garden. Corals of every colour and shade, fish of every pattern and colour palette, plankton dancing through the water in one simultaneous ballet of oceanic life. Kaia's jaw nearly dropped at this beautiful sight, stopped by her holding her breath. She looked across the underwater garden, eventually seeing a Gilled One in the distance. An old, withered looking Gilled One, with pale green skin and silver, wilted hair, dressed in what looked like a ceremonial robe.

"That's Elder Marnik. Let's go!"
Kaia nodded, following Olv towards the elder, who was feeding a school a fish around him with a content smile on his wrinkled face. He turned towards them slowly with a warm, welcoming grin.

"Fair tides to you, Prince Olv. I see you have a guest from the surface so soon. A very beautiful one, as well."

Kaia blushed and took an elegant bow in greeting.

"She must have strong lungs to be down here without a "surface tank". Truly gifted indeed."

Kaia blushed even more, her hands on her cheeks. Olv cleared his throat.

"Elder Marnik, I really hate to bother you, but I need to ask you a question. About the surface dwellers that came before her. Her parents were among them and she wants to know everything you can recall about their whereabouts and their destination."

Elder Marnik sighed deeply, a concerned look on his face.

"Hmm...Despite my kin's mistrust, I worry for those explorers. They seemed like such good-hearted creatures...but where they're going may be too much for them."

Kaia felt a rush of unease welling up inside her. She held a lump in her throat. Olv was equally nervous.

"Did they say where they were going?"

The elder paused, swallowing slowly before wording his answer.

"...They went down towards the Dark Catacombs."

Olv's skin suddenly turned pale, a terrified expression on his face.

"T-the D-Dark Catacombs?! Are you sure?!"

The elder nodded sadly. Kaia was definitely getting agitated from being out of the loop.

What's going on?! What's with these Dark Catacombs?!

They both look at the scared girl, their faces bearing a pitying expression. The Elder moved his wrinkled lips.

"The Dark Catacombs are as they sound· a labyrinth of deep, dark caves filled with countless hidden threats lurking in the old temples in which our ancestors once dwelled. They were driven out, long, long ago. Forced up to these reefs upon which we float this day, by a most dreadful creature..."

The Elder's lip quivered as he spoke the creature's name.

"The Dark Avarice."

All the Gilled Ones within earshot quivered with horror at that name, putting Kaia at risk of panic.

"The Avarice...is a gargantuan behemoth, with teeth bigger than blue whales, a body that dwarfs a reef. Ever since its arrival, our relics, which once shined brightly, have lost their light. The Avarice despises light and has an unending appetite for unfortunate prey that wander to its domain....like your parents. "

That was it. The news Kaia didn't want to hear. She knew where they were now, but where they were was the grave of many before them. If her parents ran into the Avarice...they would surely die.

Kaia clutched her chest tight, trying to avoid hyperventilation and keep her breath in, puffing her cheeks in and out, her chest sucking in and out rapidly. She wanted

"The Dark Avarice."

to cry, she didn't know what to do! What she COULD do....
against something as terrifying as the Dark Avarice?

But then she felt Olv's hands on her shoulders, clutching
her tightly. She looked up, seeing his serious face.

"Don't worry, Kaia. Your parents won't die down there."

Kaia hastily wrote on her board, her hands still shaking.

How can you be so sure?

Olv smiled, with confidence that came out of nowhere.
"Because we won't let them! We're going to save them."
The Royal Guard gasped in shock, even Chieftain Kiav
was taken aback.
"My prince, I must strongly protest. I cannot condone a
rescue from the Catacombs, especially to rescue a mere
surface dweller. Besides, the Avarice's territory has been
sealed off by a stone gate."

Olv looked at the chieftain.
"I'm not asking you, Chieftain. Kaia and I will save them,
together."
Kaia's eyes lit up with hope. If she was wasn't
underwater, her eyes would be tearing up with joy. She
hugged Olv tightly in gratitude.
"My Prince, please think this through! What would your
father say if he were to learn of your demise upon his return?
Are you willing to risk your royal blood for this...air-
breathing invader?"
Olv nodded, clenching his fists.

"I've always been too shy to open up to others, too unsure to take action on anything. Until now. I've finally found what I want to fight for, something I could never understand in the castle. I know we've only just met, but Kaia is the first friend I have ever had and I'll gladly do anything to make her smile again! So, Chieftain. If you won't help us, that's fine, I won't force you or anyone to. We'll manage on our own.

Kiav was at a loss for words, slowly bowing at his prince's words.

"Spoken just like your father. Reckless…but noble. You finally sound like a prince. Forgive my lack of faith. We will follow you."

Olv shook his head.

"No, you have a kingdom to defend. We will go alone. Just ready some equipment and have the path to the surface cleared by the time we return."

The Royal Guard saluted at his command.

"With pleasure, Prince Olv Atlon!"

As the Royal Guard sped off to fetch supplies, Kaia was left gob smacked. She struggled to think of a response as she wrote.

Thank you…Thank you so much, Olv. I can never repay you for this! But…do you have a plan?

Olv put his hand on his chin.

"The Guard will fetch an old map of the Catacombs, some lamps for markers so we don't get lost…and some weapons. We'll use the map to try and figure out where your parents would head and work our way from there."

Olv patted Kaia's head.

"Are you okay, Kaia?"

Kaia looked at him with a surprised blush, slowly nodding with a smile.

"To be honest…I'm scared out of my mind. That act before was just to get the chieftain off my back. But I think we'll be okay together, Kaia."

Kaia blushed even more, turning a deep red. Olv mistook her blush for air trouble.

"Are you low on breath?!"

Kaia snapped of it, then shook her head, saying that she's okay to Olv. But she would need air sooner or later. She held up a finger, taking out her journal again as she sat on a nearby bench. Olv watched curiously as she wrote.

Kaia's Diving Log: Entry 2
Two hours since I dived. The good news is I now have a lead on my parents. The bad news is that they're down in a place that even the Gilled Ones fear. The Dark Catacombs, where lots of dangerous creatures are said to live, but worst of all, something called the Dark Avarice. If it's as big as they say, I can't even be certain if they could still be alive. To be honest, I'm

scared witless. Or at least, I would be if I was alone.

But I have a new friend, a Gilled One named Olv, who turns out to be the Undersea Paradise's Prince. If it wasn't for him, I'd still be in that jail cell, left to drown. I'm so grateful to him. And he's kind of cute, too. I hope he isn't reading this, it's a bit embarrassing. But long story short, we're going down into the Dark Catacombs together and I've got a good feeling.

Diving Log Entry 4

Time Submerged· 02 Hours, 02 minutes, 32 seconds·

Taking their sweet time to get prepared, Kaia and Olv finally stood at a huge enclosed gate to an abyss· an abyss that would lead straight down to the Dark Catacombs. The Royal Guards stood at attention, ready to open the gate at Olv's command.

"Ready, Kaia?"

Kaia nodded with puffed cheeks, holding her spear gun with an attached flashlight on the under barrel. She looked at her wrist, which once had the bracelet that Olv bought her, but she had put it in her satchel to keep it safe until her return. Olv waved to the gatekeeper and in response the giant gate slowly slid open with a loud, rusted squeak and groan. The Royal Guards lined with a united salute to the two young souls, swimming forward and downward...to where many fear to tread.

As Kaia and Olv dove, the light from above began to fade, the pressure getting harder on Kaia's body, as she popped her eardrums to equalize the pressure. Kaia gave a thumbs up to the concerned Olv and held his hand as they dove down further. Soon, they needed their flashlights to see, as they entered a dark, spacious, bare cave, almost devoid of life. The cave gave an unnerving feel to the two, sending a shiver up Kaia's spine.

I'm kinda scared, Olv. Do you know how deep these Catacombs are?

Olv shook his head sadly. This was unknown territory to both of them. They would need to be on their highest alert. They scanned the caves vigilantly, seeing more than they bargained for. Skeletons. Old and new human bodies littered the floor, their flesh picked clean. Kaia had to hold in her scream, clamping her mouth shut with her hands. Olv turned Kaia's head away from the dead, imploring her to move on, but Kaia shook her head. Instead, she put her hands together and closed her eyes, silently uttering a prayer for the departed.

Oci Jun,

Mistress of Currents,

Nurse of Reefs,

Take these flooded souls into your warming bosom,

So that they may know peaceful rest in the infinite blue.

The Burial Rite of the Hidden Sapphire, spoken by Kaia's people to send off their dead, be they outsider or local. Kaia prayed silently to these poor people. Olv floated next to her,

"Oci Jun,

Mistress of Currents

Nurse of Reefs,

Take these flooded souls into
your warming bosom,

So that they may know peaceful
rest in the infinite blue."

joining her in prayer.
Opening their eyes, Kaia and Olv swam on, leaving the dead
to their rest. On and on they swam, the cave empty and
eerily quiet, keeping them both on edge. In silence they
swam. Olv looked at Kaia, bubbles trickling from her nose
and lips, her stomach sucked in because of the pressure. Olv
couldn't help but blush at her grace and form, but Kaia didn't
notice.

Further ahead, they swam down another sheer downward
curve, the pressure growing further as Kaia popped her ears
again. They couldn't tell how far down they were now, but
they knew they were VERY far down - further down than
most humans could on only their lungs.
Deeper and deeper they went, the cave expanding in width
until even the walls were hard to see. Still, they went down.
Finally, they saw something. Something huge. A gate of
stone and marble, spanning the whole width of the cave,
standing in their way. Kaia's eyes lit up with wonder and awe
at the sight of this underwater marvel. Olv's jaw simply
dropped.

"Did...did my ancestors make THIS? It's huuuuge!"
Kaia swam closer to the doors, far too big and heavy for them
to push open. She ran her fingers along the flat, grainy
surface of the gate, covered by runes and patterns destined to
be forgotten. Kaia reached into her satchel, pulling out her
camera again. She backed away enough to get a good view for
a photo of the runes. The camera clicked with a bright flash,
sending Olv's eyes white. The Gilled Boy wandered blindly,
disoriented from the flash.

"AGH, I can't see! What was that light?! Kaia, where are you?!"

Kaia, realizing what happened, grabbed Olv's shoulders to try and calm him. Moments later, his vision returned, his eyes refocusing to see her worried expression. Olv couldn't help but blush and look away. He laughed nervously.
"Sorry...what is that thing, anyway?"
Kaia noticed him pointing to her camera.

This is a camera. It's a device that allows one to take pictures of things and record them to be preserved in the future. I just took a photo of this thing, which we can look at any time.

Olv looked at the photo displayed on the camera, looking over it with wonder.
"Amazing. I'd love to see more devices from the surface someday, but the Royal Guard won't let me have anything. They always confiscate it."
Kaia patted Olv's head, understanding his sadness.
"But that's for another time. Now, we need to figure out how to open this gate. Hmm. There are three big slots. There must be keys somewhere....but where?"
Olv held his fingers on his chin, deep in thought. Kaia tapped Olv's shoulder, making a circling motion with her finger.

"Right. We won't find out by floating here. Let's look around. Oh, before I forget."

Olv took a lamp from his pocket. One of the lamps from Kaia's parents' crew.

"I got really curious, so I snuck one. Maybe we can leave it here so we don't get lost?"

Kaia gave a thumbs up and a smile. Hanging the lamp on a hole near the gate, they started their search for the keys to the gate. They scanned the pitch black water with their flashlights, sifting through the odd fish and the swirling dust. Eventually, they spotted a conspicuous looking hole in the barren walls that looked like it could hold something of interest. Kaia shrugged, figuring that this would be as good a place to start as any.

Olv, I'm going to take a look down here.
Could you wait here for me, please?

"Huh? Are you sure?"

Kaia nodded reassuringly, putting a hand on Olv's shoulder. Then, she swam in alone, leaving Olv to hold the front. Kaia held her spear gun at the ready, silently hoping she wouldn't have to use it. Scanning the walls with a sharp eye, she saw nothing as the cave grew suspiciously quiet. She couldn't help but feel uneasy from the emptiness, more bubbles trickling from her lips. The cave up ahead opened up, expanding to a few metres in width. Kaia swam to the centre of the open cave, looking around in all directions. She felt like she was being watched again, certain that it wasn't another Gilled One, but...something else.

She looked left, she looked right, she looked up and she looked down. She looked in every direction, trying to spot who was with her. Then she felt something on her foot.

Something smooth that stuck onto her skin. Her head tilted towards her leg.

There were tentacles. At least six long tentacles slowly wrapping around her legs, dragging her deeper into the cave despite her struggles. She wrestled the tentacles grip as they made her drop her spear gun, making moaning sounds in her throat, but she was no match for its strength. Knowing that, she stopped struggling to save her energy, trying to keep calm in spite of the danger. This wasn't her first dive, after all. The tentacles coiled around her torso, her arms, one of them even touched her puffed up cheek.
She tried to remain calm and think, but something was off. The tentacles were coiled around her, but they weren't tightening. They simply held her tight and snug, as it brought her close its head. Kaia didn't feel so threatened anymore, but rather confused. She silently wondered what this creature's intentions actually were, if not as a predator hunting its prey.

Bubbles trickled from her nose as she was dragged further into the cave, emerging into a wide spherical clearing, brightly lit up by the same green algae as the entrance way all the way back up near the surface. Not only that, but the bottom of the cave clearing was littered with artificial bits and pieces, some looking decades or even centuries old. But one piece in particular caught Kaia's eye. a glittering key of pure silver, looking a perfect match for the gate's key slots.
"Guess this wasn't a waste of air. But how do I get it?"
She thought back to her current problem. She found a key, but she couldn't reach it because she was still in the grasp of

the creature that calls this hoard home. The creature nestled around the pile, teasingly close to the key before closing its eyes to sleep. Kaia remained still, waiting and watching silently.
"If I wait until he's deep in sleep, I could slip out…!"

She had one chance at this! She could grab the key and return to Olv. As she waited, she couldn't help but think that Olv would be getting worried by now. Part of her was regretting leaving him at the entrance, yet the other part thought if they went together, they would both get caught. Shaking her head, she turned her attention back to the creature sinking into sleep.
She waited. And waited. And waited some more. But the creature's suction cups still held on tight, keeping her anchored. She struggled ever so lightly, trying to get something loose. But the slumbering creature held on tight. She waited, trying to think of something else.

"Think, Kaia. Think!"

Then she had a thought, dinging in her mind like a metaphorical lightbulb. It was a risky thought and she didn't know if it would work or not. But at this point, what choice did she have? She didn't want to risk waiting for Olv to come to her aid, only for him to get caught as well. She made up her mind and put together a plan.
She was going to pretend to drown.
Wasting no time, she started to struggle violently, shaking as much as possible to wake the creature up. As its eyes slowly opened, Kaia backed up her act by closing her eyes and

making pained moans in her throat, letting out small bursts of bubbles for added effect. Having the creature's full attention, she stopped struggling and made louder moans in her throat, puffing as much air into her cheeks as she could fit, making them flush red and round as spheres.

She made the loudest muffled moan she could make, her cheeks set to burst. Then, she let out all that air in one burst. Then…she went limp. Having one of her eyes ever so slightly open, she watched to see what the creature would do.
The creature looked at her closely, poking and stroking her limp body. As she floated weightlessly in the water, the creature grabbed her again before gently setting her down on the ground. The creature made a deep, low groan as it stroked her head. Then, at last, it swam away into its personal network, leaving her alone with the key.
As the sounds its strokes faded, she fully opened her eyes, puffing up her cheeks again. Quickly looking around, she made a break for the key. Lifting it up, it was heavier than she thought it would be, but she could still swim with it. Wasting no time, she made for the exit, trying to retrace her steps whilst silently hoping she wouldn't bump into the creature again.

At last, she could see Olv's flashlight as she found the exit. Her face lit up with relief as Olv saw her and held her in his arms, helping her with the key.
"Thank goodness you're okay. What happened in there? I was so worried!"
Kaia reached for her board, writing a hasty response.

There was a giant octopus. It caught me, but I managed to escape by fake drowning. Though it did cost me some air…

Kaia put a hand to her chest, knowing now she has less time

than before thanks to her escape plan.
"Oh, I also found a key at the bottom among the rocks while you were in there. I hope you don't mind."
Kaia's eyes lit up with a catlike smile, hugging Olv in gratitude. Wasting no more time, they slowly swam back to the gate, inserting the keys into the slots one by one, each key making a tired click. Now there was only one empty slot left.
"Two down, one to go. Let's hurry and find the last key."
Kaia nodded in agreement, swimming off with him to locate some lead, any lead that could point them to the third and final key.

Diving Log Entry 5

Time Submerged: 2 Hours, 45 Minutes, 22 seconds.

Leaving some of of their few beacons at certain points as guides through the pitch black expanse, Kaia and Olv used their flashlights to scan around, trying to find potential leads to the third and final key they need to proceed down to the Avarice's territory. As Kaia searched and Olv looked at his map, he had something on his mind.

"I'm curious. If the gate is sealed, how did your parents make it through? There are no other routes down to the deeper Catacombs, so we can't have missed them."

Kaia scratched her chin in curiousity, but she didn't have time to stop and think. She pointed forth to where her flashlight was pointing: a building formation that didn't look natural in the slightest. Built by large slabs of limestone, with a modestly sized entrance...that was mostly caved in.

They inspected the entrance, trying to find a way in amongst the messy pile of stone and rubble. Silt and sand stirred in their faces as they searched, making Kaia rub her eyes a couple of times. But amongst the dust and rubble, they found something: a small tunnel that extended under the rubble, just big enough to crawl through.

Kaia shined her flashlight down the tunnel, trying to see through the silt. She gulped and wrote on her board.

I can't see what's at the end of the tunnel. I'll have to crawl through.

Olv instantly protested.

"Kaia, no! We don't know what's in there. We don't even know if this crawlspace will hold or not. For all we know, it could collapse while you're in there!"

Kaia silently continued to write.

I know the risk and yes, it scares me. But what choice do we have? The key could be in there. We won't know unless we see for ourselves.

Olv slowly lowered his head, silently conceding. But he was coming with her, so he wouldn't have to worry as he waited. Kaia held her flashlight in her hand and reached into the crawlspace, hands first. She slowly swam inside with the utmost care, Olv following closely behind but taking care not to bump into her. Slowly they crawled, taking care not to bump the walls, for they didn't know the crawlspace's structural integrity. Silently, gradually they moved along.

Eventually, after what felt like a day of nerve-wracking care with their every move, Kaia could finally see light ahead. Her eyes lit up and she swam slightly faster. There was an exit after all. Kaia tucked in her arms and gave the water a big butterfly stroke, gliding out of the rubble.

Then she stopped dead as her head and shoulders emerged…and got stuck.

"Huh?"

That one thought popped in her head as she looked down saw her shoulders and chest stuck in the rubble and her initial confusion turned to fear. In that same moment, she felt Olv's head bump against her legs as he followed her, making her look back.

Meanwhile, Olv shined his flashlight on Kaia, seeing her legs and arms flail, trying to free herself. He quickly realized what was happening and quickly began to panic.

"OhnononononononoshesstuckwhatamIgoingtodoshesgoingtopanicanddrownandIdontknowwhattoDOOOO!"

Kaia shook her head in annoyance and kicked Olv smack-dab in the face, bringing his fit to a screeching halt. Olv shook his head, rubbing his cheek as he laughed nervously.

"Sorry, I'm a real worrywart. So, you're okay?"

Kaia gave a thumbs-up, then pointed towards the way out, then to Olv. Olv stared for a brief moment, then realized what she meant with a blush.

"You want me to give you a push??"

Kaia gave another thumbs-up.

"O-okay. Just give me a second and I'll...give you a push."

Kaia tucked her legs in, waiting for Olv to push her. While she waited, she looked around inside the structure. Judging from her first glance, this appeared to be some sort of temple. With marble walls and exotically crafted sculptures, wall carvings and scattered masonry was all around her. The resemblence to the craftsmanship in Undala Padisic was evident.

"This must have been one of their former homes before the Avarice came....I think that's what the Elder said."

Finally, she felt Olv pushing his hands against her thighs. She felt the skin on her shoulders rubbing tightly against the harsh rock, making her wince in pain, forcing a few bubbles from her lips. Olv pushed harder, but Kaia's shoulders wouldn't budge, pulling her skin harder. Kaia made a pained grunt in her throat, her eyes forced shut.

Olv pushed even harder and Kaia could finally feel her shoulders slowly starting to slip...before rocketing forward out of the gap with a pop, dragging Olv along with her. They tumbled together before settling on the dusty ground ahead, with Olv resting his chest on Kaia's lap.

Kaia looked down at Olv in surprise, who blushed furiously and swam upwards.

"Sorry! Are you okay?"

Kaia stared blankly for a moment, then nodded with a puffy cheeked smile. She then winced, clutching her shoulders as skin had blistered from her upper forearms. Olv noticed as well and swam down to her, concerned.

"You're hurt...how bad does it sting?"

Kaia winced with one eye closed, giving a reassuring smile despite the stinging pain.

"Here, hold still."

Olv slowly floated up to Kaia's blisters... and gently kissed her forearm.

Kaia felt Olv's lips on her arms, which sent a zap up her spine and hit her head with a deep red blush and a flustered twitch.

"O-o-oh please don't get the wrong idea. Our saliva mixed with the seawater makes a great healing balm."

Sure enough, Kaia looked at her blister and it was already starting to heal, her eyes widening with surprise. She smiled in gratitude.

"No problem, miss Kaia. So, are you feeling better?"

Kaia nodded, giving a thumbs up. She wrote on her board.

I owe you a lot. Thank you so much for the help out of that stick.

"Oh...no problem. So, are we on the right track?"

Kaia nodded, pointing to the familiar looking surroundings. Olv instantly recognised the architecture in a short glance.

"I think this is one of the valuable safes that the guards mentioned. They said they stored people's wealth and valuables safely further inside. This one must have been caved in when the Avarice drove everyone out. And if that's the case, then the traps might still be active."

Kaia wrote hastily.

Traps??

"Yeah. The paths to the safes are rigged with traps. If we're not careful, we could stumble into one. We should move slowly."

Kaia nodded in agreement, swallowing nervously. They both cautiously swam onwards and inwards into the abandoned halls.

The hall stretched on a few moments, before ending at an enormous locked door made of stone. There were no markings, no indents, not even a keyhole.

Then, without warning…a door behind them shut, sealing them in.

"HELLO THERE, TRAPPED VISITORS!"

A booming voice echoed through the water, seemingly from the other side of the wall.

"It's been a while and a half since I last had someone visit my vaults. But it looks like neither of ya have a vault tag! So that must mean one thing…"

The cranking and grinding of gears could be heard from the walls.

"You must be thieves, trying to steal from MY vaults. Trying to steal from me, the Forgotten Banker!"

Kaia and Olv were taken completely off guard. They weren't expecting someone else down in these abandoned depths, especially not in the buried vaults. But before any of that…

"Wait, Banker, sir! We're not thieves! We're just looking for a key to the gate!"

A moment of silence.

"I'll be the judge of that."

The door in front of them slowly rose, giving way to the

"HELLO THERE, TRAPPED VISITORS!"

path forward. But right in front of them was a huge extension of telescopic lens, glaring right at them. A tired, red eye could be seen through the lens as it surveyed them from head to toe.

"Hmm…well…you certainly don't look dressed like thieves. The only loot bag I see is that little pouch on the one with the big cheeks. Doubt you can carry much in that, though."

Kaia pointed to herself questioningly.

"Yes, you. What are you, exactly? Even I can tell you're not a Gilled One. A curious look indeed."

Kaia wrote hastily on her board.

I'm a human. My name's Kaia.

"Hmm…a human, huh?"

A raspy laugh echoed through the walls.

"That's a good one. We all know humans can't breathe underwater. And I don't see any of that gear you usually wear. So if you ARE a human, how come you aren't…uh…what do they say…drowning? Yeah, drowning, that's it."

Kaia scribbed a much lengthier answer on her board.

I'm what you'd call a special case. I can hold my breath for hours. But I need to hurry and find my parents deeper down, or soon I will need air.

Kaia clasped her hands in a pleading manner.

Please, Mr Banker. If you have a key to the gate, please, let us have it. We will never trouble you again. We promise.

A gruff, pondering huff from the Banker, followed by a moment of silence.

"A key, you say. You mean the one those outsiders hours before carelessly left in front of the gate? Hmmm...very well. I'll give you two a chance to prove yourselves. But ONLY one chance, so make it count. Listen carefully and do what I say if you want to leave here. Swim out of line and you're shark bait!"

There was no need for any discussion. They both nodded without hesitation.

"Swim forward to the vault hub. Then stop."

Kaia and Olv swam straight ahead, emerging from the decrepit halls into a huge, awe-inspiring expanse of vaults, as high as five storeys. Some were blocked by rubble, others had ruined doors that had fallen off their hinges, while others were still shut. Each vault was locked behind a secondary barred door, green with moss.

"I see you two right there. Now...stay right where you are. I'm going to put you two through a test."

They looked around the vaults in wonder and curiosity, not moving from their spots.

"Now, I'm going to offer some items. But you can only take one. Choose wisely, or you won't be leaving.

Understand?"

They both nodded instantly.

"Alright. First choice."

From above, a chained table slowly lowered from the ceiling, stopping in front of the two. On the table, were two items. One was what looked like some sort of grenade, but what kind they were unsure. The other was a beautiful, flawlessly cut sapphire, which made Kaia's eyes glitter with awe.

Her hand reached forward by itself towards the sapphire. But Olv grabbed her wrist.

"Kaia, wait. We're being tested, remember? Let's think this through."

Kaia looked at her hand, then at Olv, realizing what she almost did, the guilt hitting her like a brick wall, especially since Olv already bought her something similar. She held his hand and bowed in apology. Olv blushed, scratching the back of his head.

"Oh, it's okay. Don't worry about it. Now let's look at this, okay?"

Kaia nodded with a determined smile.

"Okay, we know about the sapphire. But this....hmmm, I think this is, if I'm not mistaken, a flash bomb."

Kaia looked at the flash bomb with curiosity. She glanced with Olv and they both knew that would be useful, especially in the darker depths, where the local creatures would be susceptible to light. Thy nodded in unison, taking the flash bomb.

The table raised back upwards with a clickety-click from the chains.

"You have chosen...wisely. But don't get cocky."
The table lowered once again, with new items on the table. This time, three items. One was an exotic gold figurine, the second was an old jewelbox, the third was another, more rectangular looking grenade.
"Okay, we know what to pick this time, Kaia."
Kaia was scribbling something on her board, more bubbles triclikng from her nose.

I just hope we don't have to use it. Explosives underwater are really bad for me.

Olv frowned in worry.
"What do you mean?"

Explosives release shock waves. When a shock wave from an explosive hits a human who's holding their breath like I am, it will hurt my insides.

Kaia went slightly pale as she wrote her next sentence.

It might even kill me.

Olv went as pale as Kaia after seeing that. They no

longer wanted to take the grenade. But they were being tested. They had no choice. Kaia took the grenade and put it in her pouch ever so deftly.

The table raised upwards once again.

"You know the risks. I could tell from your faces. You're pretty good."

The table lowered once more.

"Last test. Each of you take one."

There were four items. But that was the thing. They were all in identical looking dark green bags.

"You can't look inside until you've chosen. This one is purely on instinct. See if you can pick the right ones."

Kaia and Olv looked intensely at the bags, searching for some sort of difference. Kaia poked the left most bag. It felt solid and heavy, so she ruled that one out. Olv felt the right most one. It felt totally empty. The center two felt like they had something inside them, but they couldn't tell what.

"Which ones do we pick?"

Kaia scratched the back of her head, thinking long and hard about her options. She couldn't tell what was in the middle two bags, but she knew the ones on the right were lighter than the ones on the left. She looked at Olv.

"I'm not sure, to be honest Kaia. What do you think?"

Kaia pointed to the two bags on the right.

They're the lightest.

Olv slowly nodded in agreement.

"Good point, I was thinking something similar."

There was a long moment of silence.

"Ready to take the chance?"

Kaia slowly nodded in a trusting smile. Kaia grabbed one and Olv grabbed the other. And with that, the table raised a final time.

"Alright. You may look inside your bags."

Kaia looked in the right most bag she picked and sure enough, it was empty. Olv looked in his and found a small necklace in the shape of a cresent moon. It was pearl white with a dim shine.

"Alright, I think that's proof enough that you two aren't thieves. That empty bag can be useful for something you might find. That amulet can be used to blind critters in really dark places, when the flash bomb won't cut it. But it stopped glowing when the Dark Avarice showed up. The other two bags had treasures which you refused. As for the key you're after, I'll fetch it for you. Stay right there."

Their faces lit up with triumph, especially Kaia, who was all giddy with joy and relief. She held up her hand for a high five, which Olv hit happily.

"We did it, Kaia! We make such a great team!"

Kaia smiled happily behind her puffed cheeks, clutching their prizes happily. As they celebrated, the table lowered once again, this time holding something familiar; the sapphire from before and better yet, the third key they were searching for.

"This is the one you're looking for, yeah? The sapphire is a thank you bonus, for your courtesy."

Olv eagerly took the key in his hands, whilst Kaia took the sapphire and bowed deeply gratitude before writing.

Thank you so much. What could we do to repay you?

The Banker huffed at her graceful thanks.

"Hmm, there's one thing I need you to do, if possible. If you promise me this, I'll open the way out to you."

They both nodded instantly.

"Ah, thanks. When you go back up to see the others, could you...tell them I'm still here? I've been trapped...Well, I've CHOSEN to be trapped here for quite a while. Someone's gotta look after it all, right?"

Kaia and Olv looked at each other and both nodded with a smile.

"Heh...thanks, kids. I'll open the emergency exit for you. Best of luck, you two."

A rumble could be heard all the way back at the entrance, which made Kaia's and Olv's heads turn. As the telescopes withdrew and the speakers fell silent, they felt it was time to move on. They swam back to the entrance to discover a small opening beside the collapsed entryway. They stroked a steady pace through the clear, empty exit before once again, emerging into the dark, expanding dead waters before the great gate...final key in hand.

Diving Log Entry 6

Time Submerged. 3 Hours, 02 Minutes, 33 Seconds.

Kaia and Olv once again floated before the great gate locked by the Gilled Ones to seal off the creature known as the Dark Avarice. Only opened once before...by Kaia's parents.

As Olv hoisted the key in his hands towards the gate, Kaia wrote another journal entry.

Kaia's Diving Log: Entry 3
Just over three hours since I dove and I can only feel the slightest tingle in my chest. Sooner or later, I WILL need to surface. I can only hope the exit will be clear on my way up.
So far, we've come across a huge gate we needed three keys to open. My friend Olv found one on the ground, I found the second key in what I think was a squid's den. Or an octopus, I'm not sure. In any case, I had to pretend to drown to get free from it. Not going to lie, my cheeks are

getting a bit sore.

The last key was in an abandoned Gilled One's vault hub, run by a guy called the Forgotten Banker. He tested us, by making us choose certain stuff to prove we weren't thieves, including a sticky timed grenade, a once-glowing amulet and a flash bomb. He also gave me a beautiful sapphire as a thank you gift in exchange for letting the other Gilled Ones know about him. I'll treasure this little gem and all the precious people I've met.

We're about to open the gate now. Mom, Dad...

I'm coming.

Kaia put her journal away as Olv slotted in the final key, all three turning in unison. The gate rumbled heavily, shaking the very water around it as it slowly slid open, revealing a vast void ahead.

Kaia swallowed nervously. From this point they were in the Dark Avarice's territory. All they could do was pray they don't see it. Olv looked at Kaia nervously.

"R-ready?"

Kaia slowly nodded, just as anxious as him as she reached for his hand. Forward they swam together, hand in

Mom...Dad...

I'm coming.

hand into the dangerous void…

The cave opened outwards and downwards until they couldn't see the walls anymore. They weren't in a cave anymore, they were in an abyss. Their flashlights didn't illuminate anything as they went straight downwards. As they descended, both of them, especially Kaia, began to understand the danger of where they were and what they were doing.

Kaia pinched her nose and popped her ears again to equalize the growing pressure. Olv couldn't help but marvel at this special girl. Most humans wouldn't make it down to this depth, especially on one breath. Even if they could, the pressure and freezing temperature could kill them. But not Kaia. All the sub-freezing water did to Kaia was make her shiver occasionally.

Kaia caught Olv staring at her, making him recoil with a blush. She gave a mischievous smirk, wanting to investigate this briefly. She wrote on her board.

Olv, what are you curious about me?

Olv looked at her smiling face, as if it was shining.

"I-I'm just curious about you, Kaia. N-not just as a human, but as a person. I don't know why, but I want to know more about you. It's what I want more than anything in these seas."

Now it was Kaia's turn to blush beet red. Coupled with her puffed up cheeks, it made Olv chuckle.

"Plus you are kind of….cute."

Kaia covered her face with her hands. A lot of people called her "tough", "strong", "brave" and "talented". But that was the first time in a long while someone called her "cute." She didn't know how to react...

...Apart from squealing internally.

But this did help break the tension they were in, which made them both feel at least a more at ease. Holding hands again, they continued downwards.

But they were not ready for what they saw.

Teeth. Gargantuan, jagged red teeth that stretched as high as an apartment and as wide as a street, coming towards Kaia and Olv at an alarming speed. In a split second, both their hearts nearly leaped out of their chests and Kaia had to hold in her terrified scream. There was no time to think. They had to flee.

They swam away as fast as they could, not even daring to look back at the maw chasing them.

"That-that must be the Dark Avarice! QUICK! We need to find somewhere to-"

But before Olv could finish their sentence, they saw the same teeth chasing them, in front of them coming together with a thunderous thud. And then...

Complete darkness.

Olv tossed and rolled out of control in the darkness, trying to find his flashlight.

Click.

His flashlight lit up once more, bringing a brief relief. But it didn't last long once he saw where he was. He looked around and all his light illuminated were teeth, gums and an enormous, brown tongue.

"That thing.....ate us!"

Looking around more, Olv quickly realized an even bigger problem.

Kaia was nowhere in sight. Olv quickly began to panic.

"Kaia?! KAIA!! KAIA, WHERE ARE YOU?!"

Frantically he called out frantically for Kaia, but the only response was the deep, low growls of the creature that held them in its jaws.

"KAIA!"

He searched everywhere, anywhere, trying to find some kind of lead to her location.

"KAIA!"

He kept calling out, his voice starting to crack as despair began to set in.

"Kaia…! Please…"

He stopped dead in the water, on the edge of utter defeat.

"Kaia…please tell me you're okay…"

He was on the edge of tears. Tears that would never be seen in the ocean. He called out one last time.

"KAIA DON"T LEAVE ME ALL ALONE!"

Silence. Utter, still, silence.

Hopeless, staring blankly through his clouded eyes, Olv saw something. A faintest of lights, in the darkest of places.

He swam towards it without a hint of hesitation, holding onto his last sliver of hope. He got closer and closer until it shined into his eyes. His heart slowed to a relieved pace. It was a mounted flashlight on a speargun. And next to it, Kaia huddled into a ball on the jaw lining.

He slowly swam towards her, ever so slowly, his own eyes and heart welling up with hope. He touched her shoulder softly.

Kaia's head bolted upward in shock, her eyes wide with horror. When she saw Olv, her eyes welled up with invisible tears and held Olv in a tight, relieved embrace. They both broke down in each other's arms.

"Kaia, thank the currents you're okay! I thought I lost you!"

Olv blubbered, his voice cracking in sadness. Kaia nodded back and hugged him tight, unable to talk, unable to hold back her fear. She messily wrote on her board.

I'm so scared! What are we going to do?

Olv held Kaia's shoulders softly.

"Shhh. Its okay, Kaia. We'll think of something. Let's just…stop and think."

They both sat down on the gums, each deep in their own thoughts. Kaia put one hand on her chest, steadying her heart and holding Olv's hand tightly with the other, who squeezed back as his mind went into overdrive. They looked around, scanning the pitch black waters with their flickering flashlights, trying to think of something, anything.

Olv then looked at Kaia's face. Her dark, wavy hair drifted elegantly in the water, her tanned skin shining from the flashlight, her puffed up cheeks showing a faint hint of redness and her gleaming sapphire blue eyes wide with worry. Despite the situation they were in, he just couldn't help but stare, being this close to her. He didn't know why before.

He did now.

"Kaia…"

He swallowed deeply, gently putting his hand on her cheek and turning her head towards him. Her eyes gazed deeply into his, making the water around them grow silent and still.

"I won't leave you all alone again. Ever. I'll get us out of this somehow, rescue your parents and get you some fresh air."

He held her hands tight.

"You are not drowning on my watch."

Kaia could only stare at him, his face stiff with newfound courage in the face of dire crisis. She slowly put her hand on his face, giving him the purest of smiles. She didn't need to say anything, her face said it all.

"Thank you, Olv."

With newfound courage and regained nerves, they both

clutched their spearguns.

"I think it's time we finally put these to use."

Kaia nodded, pointing to the gums they were sitting, where the creature giant teeth stuck out. She wrote a plan.

If we shoot between the teeth and gums, that will hurt it and make it open it's mouth.

Olv looked uncertain.

"Are you sure that will work?"

Trust me, I've been to the dentist. Besides, we have to at least try!

"Alright…What's a "den…tist?"

Kaia face palmed. Way to kill the mood, she thought silently.

Kaia took aim at the top of the monsters gums, aiming between two molars. They both only had one shot, so she had to get this right. She closed her eyes, slowing her heart and focusing her mind. Olv took aim at the teeth to the right of where Kaia was aiming, waiting for her to fire.

A long moment of silence….until finally…

"NOW!"

Kaia pulled the trigger, sending the spear shooting through the water, right in between the teeth. Olv fired in succession. They could hear the spears burrowing through the gaps and striking the squishy nerves below.

"Bingo."

A deafening roar rattled their ears as the Avarice's jaws snapped open, roaring in pain. Seeing the gap, they wasted no time swimming for freedom. As the monster flailed and raged, the two swam out from its monstrous jaws, swimming downwards amidst the chaos.

Among the dust and falling rocks, they needed to find shelter from its destructive path. Olv pulled Kaia into a sheltered cave opening as a falling shoulder was about to pin her. In the act, he pulled her very close to him, making them both blush upon realization. Kaia scratched her head with a red hue on her face.

"Thanks, Olv. You really saved my butt there."

"Oh, n-no problem. I'm just glad your plan paid off. Nice thinking, Kaia."

The Avarice shot upwards, towards the entrance from which Kaia and Olv came from. They were safe from the debris for the time being.

"Right…so what do we do now?"

As Olv asked, Kaia saw a faint image further in the cave. Her body moved forward by itself.

"Hey, Kaia! Where are you going?"

Kaia didn't stop. Olv swam frantically to try and catch up. As they dove further and further, the faintest of lights flickered at the end. It was an artificial light, Kaia knew this.

They emerged from the cave. They found it. A "Regal

Glider" submarine. The very same one designed by her father. And it was Model 01, piloted by Victor and Lia Cayden, Kaia's parents.

It was a flooded wreck. Her parents were nowhere to be seen. Kaia's heart began to race uncontrollably as she frantically searched everywhere inside and outside the sub. Olv could only watch her desperation as he too realized.

"Kaia? Is this…your parents' vessel?"

She searched everywhere. Nothing. Only photos and memories. She sank into the open cockpit, reality hitting her like an anvil as she huddled in utter defeat.

Olv swam into the cockpit, ever so gently putting his hand on her shoulder as she silently wept. She wrote slowly with one hand.

They're…gone, Olv. They're not here. They're…

Kaia didn't want to write that next word. But her hand moved on its own, facing the cold dark reality.

Dead.

She dropped her pen, letting her board fall to the floor. She hanged her head in grief, silently mourning her loss.

Olv didn't want to believe it either, but even he knew that humans couldn't survive for long at this depth, except for Kaia. But they weren't Kaia. He surveyed the scenario as he thought it may have happened. They might have run into

They're...gone, Olv.
They're not here.
They're....

Dead.

the Dark Avarice, who damaged their sub and forced them to crash here, and…

His thoughts stopped there. He didn't want to dwell on it. He just wanted to help Kaia. Olv looked around the cockpit, seeing photos of her family, all smiling and happy as she grew up. Seeing their smiles in these soaked, faded images made him understand completely what her parents meant to her.

"Kaia. I'm so sorry."

Kaia and Olv held each other tight in each other's arms as they silently wept in the last lingering traces of her family…lost in the deep, unforgiving blue. It felt like hours they huddled together in quiet solitude before Kaia softly clutched Olv's chest. She stared in his eyes, hers full of pain.

"Kaia, what do you want to do now? Whatever it is, I will follow."

Olv softly held her hands in his. She thought for the longest moment, before she reached for her board that she dropped. She slowly wrote.

I want to be with my parents. More than anything.

Olv's heart quickened in a blink at her next words.

Olv, will you stay here, with me….until then?

For the first time he knew what a breaking heart felt like. He knew what she wanted, but he wasn't at all ready for it. Yet he couldn't refuse her request. Painfully, grief clutching his heart and soul, he slowly nodded.

"….Okay. I'll be right here. Until Oci Jun comes. But…"

Olv's lip quivered heavily.

"Before you go…I want to know everything about you. So I can remember you for who you are, not as I thought you were."

Kaia nodded, her mind and conscience clear. With that, she started to write the biggest wall of text her board could fit. Olv took a similar board and copied her every word.

My name is Kaia Cayden. I'm from a little island called Loa in the Hidden Sapphire Archipelago. My mother was one of the best divers in the islands. Her name was Lia. My father was an ocean scientist from another country called Sweden, far away from here. His name was Victor Cayden. They loved each other so much they eventually had me.

Olv copied every word before Kaia erased her board and started anew.

They first found out about my breath hold when I was four years old. I dived to the bottom of the pool all by myself and stayed under for over 30 minutes. I obviously got in trouble for scaring them, but they were also happy for me. After that, they let me swim a lot more. I loved swimming every day. I loved diving every day. I loved being in the ocean every single day. I hoped for that one day I would go into the ocean and never have to leave.

Kaia's face flushed red as the growing need for air reared its head. She put a hand to her chest, wincing for a moment.

I met all sorts of kids as I grew up, some even trying to bully me or those I liked. I usually pulled a prank on them which involved pretending to drown and getting them in trouble, but only ever as a last resort. But despite me being as friendly as I could, I could never make any REAL friends because they all were scared they couldn't keep up with me, while others just didn't like me. I got really lonely. My only friends... were the fish. They loved me as much as I loved them.

Kaia took a long moment for this next line and she looked Olv in the eye as she wrote it.

As much as I love you, Olv.

Olv's face went beet red, his pencil fumbling in his fingers out of sheer shock. He could only muster a nervous laugh.

"Heh hehe, g-g-good one, Kaia. Wait…you…you ARE joking, right?"

Kaia shook her head with complete certainty. She wasn't joking.

"Oh."

That was all Olv could muster, with a stunned expression. Kaia smiled warmly and hugged him closer than ever, her red, puffed up cheek pressing up against his. Olv gently reached and patted her long hair, feeling her soft strands run through his fingers. She loved this young Gilled One. And this Gilled One loved her.

"Kaia…am I a real friend?"

There were no words needed. He felt her chin nod against his shoulder. Olv's heart warmed up and his eyes began to tear up. His courage began to crumble as his voice cracked.

"Kaia…I'm so scared. I don't want you to go."

Kaia's chest slightly heaved from the mammalian reflex, her body trying to force her to breathe. But she held on.

"Kaia…I don't want you to go…I don't want you to leave."

Kaia clutched Olv tight, the pain in her chest slowly growing.

"Kaia…You're my first true friend too. I love you."

A spark lit in Kaia's soul from those words. Her eyes opened wide, a red blush running across her face. She pulled back from her embrace, looking Olv dead in the eyes. Her face asked the question without any words.

"Say that one more time."

Olv was taken aback for a moment, but managed to muster up some words.

"I-I love you, Kaia. You're not only b-b-beautiful….b-b-b-b but you're very kind…and you can hold your breath for a very long time…which means you can spend more time with me."

He put his hands on her shoulders firmly.

"I want to know you myself. Which is why I've made my choice. I won't let you drown here. Not in this hellhole. Even if your parents are gone, I'm still here. And I want to be with you more and more."

Kaia was at a complete loss for words. Her stunned expression said it all.

"I love you too much to lose you, Kaia! I'll say it as many times as you need me too. I love you! I love you more than I love breathing! I lo-"

Kaia put a finger to Olv's lip, silencing him with the warmest smile.

Olv…Thank you.

Kaia's eyes lit up with newfound hope, hugging Olv. Olv patted her back in return, almost shedding an invisible tear to see Kaia smile again.

"Okay, first things first, we need to get up to the surface. But the Avarice is still up there and I'll bet it won't just let us swim along with a wave goodbye. We'll need to do somet-"

A bell rang in Olv's head. He had an idea.

"Kaia, I've got it. It's a really dangerous and frankly, stupid idea but if it works, it'll help us and my people."

It didn't take long for Kaia to give an answer.

What choice do we have? Let's do it.

Olv knew from her answer how much she trusted him. There was nothing else for it. They had to act quick, for Kaia had little time left.

"Alright, here's the plan. We'll need the stuff we got from the Forgotten Banker, the right timing and all the swimming strength we have."

Kaia listened closely.

Diving Log Entry 7

Time Submerged. ?? Hours, ?? Minutes, ?? seconds

The Dark Avarice, gargantuan in size and with its own voracious appetite, stalked the dark waters, guarding the only way out. It's enormous form a mystery to those who still draw breath, it's a wonder it managed to move around in this isolated cave network. It bode its time despite the pain in its gums, waiting for prey to stave off its hunger.
It didn't have to wait long.

"HEY!! BARNICLE BRAINS!"

The Avarice heard a small voice and slowly turned around, eyeing its next meal. The meal in question being a little Gilled One named Olv. He floated in the middle of the water, barely managing to hide his fear. The Avarice grinned and shot straight for him, mouth agape...unaware of what it was swimming into.
Olv swam away in terror as the Avarice gave chase, but it was quickly catching up. Opening up its jaws, about to swallow the Gilled One again and this time for good. But Olv pulled the flash grenade out of his pocket, pulled the pin and tossed it before turning away and covering his ears.

BANG!

An ear-piercing bang echoed violently through the water, along a with a blinding white flash that rang the Avarice's eardrums and whited out its eyes, rending it temporarily deaf and blind, sending it into an aimless, flailing rage. The Avarice smashed the walls of the cavern in every direction, making it rumble violently, shaking the rocks above loose, crashing down on it's body. In the midst of all this chaos, Kaia swam quietly along the rumbling ceiling of the cave, executing her part of the plan. Putting the explosives on a timer, stick them on the rocks and get out of there. The rumbling of the Avarice's rampage made this especially tricky as she tried to fumble with the bomb's fine mechanics. With a click and a steady tick, Kaia swam like away as fast as she could, heading straight back to Olv.

At this point, the Avarice was starting to regain it's senses, its sight and hearing returning to normal, despite a few heavy rocks weighing its body down. The ravenous creature glared at the two with livid eyes, baring its enormous teeth as it reared to strike.

Then Olv looked at Kaia.

"Kaia, get behind me!"

She did.

The Avarice gathered its strength to pounce, already licking its lips with its ghastly tongue. There was nowhere for the two to run or hide. They were floating ducks.

Or so it thought.

Because it was at that moment, an almighty roar echoed directly above the Avarice as the bomb detonated, sending half the cave crashing down on its body. It flailed and struggled against the falling debris, roaring in agony and anger...before falling still and silent, releasing a final breath.

They had done it! They beat the Dark Avarice. Kaia and Olv hugged in triumph, their hearts still racing from the adrenaline rush, the biggest smiles on their faces. Olv felt woozy from taking the shockwave for the explosion, but he knew it was better for him to take it than her. Kaia held him worriedly, but he smiled and bared the pain, patting her head to reassure her.

Then, as if in congratulations, the dull amulet around Kaia's neck suddenly started to glow brightly, illuminating the entire dark cavern, including what could be seen of the Dark Avarice's dark, scaly body that wasn't buried under a heap of rock. The amulet also revealed another path. One that was completely unseen before.

Kaia swam towards it on instinct alone. She felt something she couldn't quite put her finger on, but she had to find out, despite the growing pain in her lungs. Straight down she swam, the amulet leading the way.

"Kaia! Where are you going? The exit's that way!"

Olv swam after Kaia, wondering what she's looking for down there and worrying about her dwindling breath. But he followed her regardless. As they swam, they saw a faint light in the distance. An artificial light. One that was strikingly familiar to Kaia. She got closer and she recognised it instantly.

Six anchored pods. Pods that were launched from Victor Cayden's "Regal Gliders". They were all lit and all intact. Kaia's face was glowing with joy and without even a thought,

she swam to the windows of the pods. Through each
window, she saw a familiar face, looking back at her in shock
and surprise, letting the others know who they just saw.
After their initial shock, they wave back at her with a hopeful
smile, then pointing to the other pods. Olv also introduced
himself as well, receiving a more curious look from the crew,
much to his embarrassment.

Kaia looked through the other pod windows, seeing more of
the crew alive and well, yet trapped. The last pod offered the
biggest surprise of all.
Lia and Victor Cayden, Kaia's parents, were alive and well.
She put her hand against the window, seeing them notice her
with parental shock. Shocked that their daughter was all the
way down in these dangerous depths holding her breath, but
glad they could see her face again. She took out her board
and wrote to her parents, wanting to cry in joy.

*Mom! Dad! I missed you so much. I thought
I lost you.*

They both put their hands against the window as well,
sharing her feelings. They missed her too. Olv couldn't bring
himself to interrupt their tender reunion, so he sat and
watched silently. But the moment didn't last long anyway, for
Kaia had suddenly exhaled a big cloud of bubble before
instinctively covering her mouth with both hands.
Kaia was running out of breath, fast. She had no time to
chat.
Her parents saw her distress, their faces heavy with worry.
Victor frantically searched and found a board to write on as
well.

Kaia, our air is running low as well, our filters are
busted. But you can help. Unclip the anchors at the
bottom of the pods and we can float back up to
the surface, given the path is clear. You can hitch
on the last pod so you don't have to swim. Just
push the lock and pull the chain out, okay?

Kaia nodded, her face red with strain. Wasting no time, she
swam underneath her parent's pod, wanting to release them
first. Luckily, unclipping the anchors was as easy as her
father said and sure enough, with a bubbly click, the pod
floated upwards towards the way they came, steering
towards the surface.
One down, five to go. Olv helped Kaia unclipping the other

pods to ease her burden. One by one, the pods floated upwards to freedom. Until the last pod. She pushed the lock, but it wouldn't move enough for the chain to get free. The lock was jammed shut. There was nothing for it. She had to use brute force to break the chain free. Olv took the chain and pulled along with her with everything he had. With every second Kaia pulled, her face grew steadily redder and more strained. She wasn't leaving anyone behind, even to her last breath.
Then, finally.

SNAP.

The chain snapped in their hands, setting the final pod free floating upwards. But Kaia recoiled and let go of the chain, leaving her and Olv alone at the bottom.
Kaia's parents were saved, but she wasn't out of the woods yet. She had to face her biggest problem yet, her breath. Seeing her strain as she covered her nose and mouth, Olv took matters into his own arms, as well as Kaia herself. Carrying her upwards and swimming at full speed so Kaia could focus on holding what little fresh air she left, her cheeks turning a light blue, her stomach sucking in. The amulet around Kaia's neck lighting the way, Olv swam straight up as fast as he could, determined to get her all the way back to the surface.
As she held desperately, she thought to herself...

"What if I don't make it?"

With those dark thoughts in her mind, she got out her

journal to write one last entry. Writing with one hand, holding her nose and mouth with the other, she shakily wrote as Olv carried her upwards.

Kaia's Diving Log: Entry 4 (Final Entry)
To Mom and Dad
As I'm writing this, I'm struggling to hold my breath. It hurts so much, my body is screaming for me to breathe. But I want to write this last entry in case I don't make it. If that's the case, a Gilled boy named Olv will get this to you.
Olv is my friend. He's been with me this entire dive. He got me out of jail, he helped me find out where you guys went, he helped me find and get help from the Forgotten Banker, and he even saved me...when I lost all hope. We even beat the Dark Avarice together. If it wasn't for Olv, I wouldn't have made it this far. I like him so much. I love him. He's my first true friend. I want to be with him more. I want to see him more. I want to play with him more.

A big cloud of stale air forced itself from Kaia's mouth.

But I'm so scared...My hearts racing, my cheeks are bulging and sore...My lungs are

screaming....
Mom...Dad...If I don't make it...

I'm sorry.

I love you.

Kaia

Kaia shakily closed her journal for the last time, putting it in her back pocket. Passing the Forgotten Bank and heading back up towards the Undersea Paradise, her face turned less beet red and more airless blue as she groaned from the strain. Natural light returned to the pair's eyes as they reached the Undersea Paradise's open gates, surprised by a momentous cheer from the masses that called this place home. As they swam through the gates, the Royal Guard kneeled in respect, the Chieftain front and center.
"My Prince, you have returned...and by our dull relics glowing once more, you managed to slay the Avarice! You truly are a brave Prince worthy of the crown."

The Chieftain hanged his head.
"I am ashamed to have doubted you. Allow me to redeem myself by arranging a great celebration!"
The masses cheered. But Olv had someone else on his mind.
"That sounds great, but can it wait? Kaia needs air, now! I need to carry her to the surface! Is the path clear?!"

The chieftain was suddenly less enthusiastic.

"Well, yes. And the others in their vessels passed by some
time ago. But...your people need you now."
Olv was outraged for his lack of concern for his suffering
friend.
"Are you serious?! My friend's about to drown! I-"
Kaia patted Olv's shoulder, shakily writing on her board.

*It's okay, Olv. I can swim the rest of the way.
I don't know if I can make it...*

But in case I don't...

Kaia put her hands gently on Olv's face...

...and innocently kissed his lips.

Olv went beet red, his eyes wide with shock. Kaia was the one holding her breath, but Olv felt breathless. The people around gasped with surprise, followed by stunned silence. Kaia had no spare time left. With a reluctant wave goodbye, she bade farewell to her Gilled friends and swam for the exit with everything she had. Olv reluctantly joined the other Gilled Ones, watching her leave, unsure if he would ever see her again.

Kaia put on a brave face for Olv and his people, but she was soon regretting it as by the time she passed the now cleared blockage, nearly all of her remaining air was welled up in her cheeks, trying to get out. She moaned in agony as she swam at full speed, her eyes barely open from the strain.
Past the algae, past the wreckage, out of the entrance and finally, up where the anchor once laid. Every familiar sight felt like an eternity to pass between. Kaia's arms and legs were burning, but she didn't dare slow down. Her face was deep blue, her cheeks round with stale air and her eyes were forced shut as she swam straight up for dear life.

She couldn't see the surface. Her body was screaming at her in her head.

"BREATHE, KAIA! BREATHE!"

She tried to block it out, but her air forced its way out her lips in a long, continuous stream. Her lungs were at her limit, emptying out by force. She needed air, now.
The surface was in sight, the sunlight rippled through the

water onto her skin, the currents brushed through her hair and through her eyes opened just a crack, she saw the six pods floating on the surface.
Her arms went numb, her legs went numb, her lungs were nearly empty....

But it didn't matter.

At the absolute limit of what her
body could muster…

Kaia breached the surface, taking the biggest breath of air she'd ever taken in her life.
The crew saw her flailing in the water, gasping desperately and threw a life preserver her way. She held onto it, colour returning to her face as she caught her breath. They reeled her in, hoisting her on board and checking on her for any medical requirements. A middle-aged male from the crew held Kaia's shoulder, trying to keep her awake.

"Miss Kaia, are you okay? Are you hurt anywhere?"
She slowly shook her head, just catching her breath.
"I'm.....okay.....just.......tired....."
She spoke weakly between her breaths.
"Are...Mom.....and...Dad.....okay?"

The crew smiled in gratitude and wonder at this little girl's selflessness and bravery.
"Yes, they're okay. We're all okay...thanks to you."
Kaia smiled at the good news, her eyelids getting heavy.
"Good....I can.... see...Mom...Dad... and Olv...again...."

With that, Kaia passed out, exhausted. And no-one could blame her. The crew found her journal as she slept, finding what she wrote while she was down there. They also found the amulet around her neck, along with the sapphire wristband in her satchel. Victor and Lia saw their heroine and miracle of a daughter, sleeping soundly and softly after diving to the depths of the Sunken Mazes, discovering the Undersea Paradise and the Gilled Ones, saving the Forgotten

Banker, slaying the Dark Avarice, rescuing her parents and
their crew and most of all, making her first true friend.
And she did all of this...

In One Breath.

THE END...

www.ingramcontent.com/pod-product-compliance
Lightning Source LLC
Chambersburg PA
CBHW070629120726
47909CB00004B/1368